The Tangled Loon

by Virginia Cassarino-Brown

illustrated by Dawn Leeman Prindall

Goose River Press
Waldoboro, ME 04572

Library of Congress Control Number: 2011940659

ISBN 978-1-59713-118-6

First Printing, 2011

Published by
Goose River Press
3400 Friendship Road
Waldoboro, ME 04572
e-mail: gooseriverpress@roadrunner.com
www.gooseriverpress.com

The Tangled Loon

To my husband Allan Brown, whose experience with a tangled loon inspired this story. You really are the loon whisperer!

Also, to my mother the late Jean Cella Cassarino, who shared her love of books and reading to generations of children. I was lucky enough to be one of them!

–Virginia Cassarino-Brown

To my family, the best on earth, with a special call out to Gram Grace, who is 94 and an experienced reader of countless children's books to many generations of kids. I predict *The Tangled Loon* will be her new favorite.

–Dawn Leeman Prindall

Jason scrambles down the grassy hill and races toward the lake. Along the way he picks up a smooth flat rock. He turns it over in his palm a few times and realizes that he just found a perfect skipping stone. *I wonder how many jumps I'll get out of this one?* he says to himself.

The mountains on the horizon are alight in a soft purple glow. The water is calm and the air is still. He is enjoying a beautiful summer evening on the shore of Mooselookmeguntic, a lake nestled in the western mountains of Maine. He leans back into his step and flings the rock into the water, watching it skim across the surface.

"Ten! Ten skips! My new record!" he yells to his elderly neighbor, Mr. Brown, who is rowing by in his old wooden boat looking none too pleased by the disturbance.

"Hey, Mr. Brown, whatcha doin'?" Jason calls to the old man.

"I'm tryin' to find some peace and quiet." Mr. Brown continues to pull on the oars of his withered boat. He closes his eyes, and inhales deeply. A faint splash about the water stirs him.

"Stop throwing those blasted stones into the lake, kid," he yells to Jason.

"It's not me, Mr. Brown," Jason replies. "It's a loon!"

Jason notices the distinctive bird with its geometrical black and white plumage swimming and diving, swimming and diving, each time resurfacing closer to Mr. Brown. He is puzzled. The young boy knows that loons don't behave that way. They're shy. They NEVER let people get near them. They're kind of like Mr. Brown. He watches the loon glide up to the edge of the boat. All of a sudden, he sees his neighbor reach over the side and firmly grab onto the loon, wrapping his boney fingers around the loon's neck!

"Heeyyyyy!" Jason yells. "Whatcha doin'? Whatcha doing to that loon?" The young boy frantically waves his arms over his head and tries to get the old man's attention.

"Stop your squawking. Can't you see I'm busy?" Jason watches Mr. Brown continue to hold onto the bird. He just can't understand why the loon seems calm in the old man's hold. *Why isn't the bird trying to get away?* "What's wrong?" he yells to Mr. Brown.

Finally, the old neighbor responds. "Make yourself useful kid. Bring me some scissors. This loon is tangled up in fishing line and I can't save her on my own."

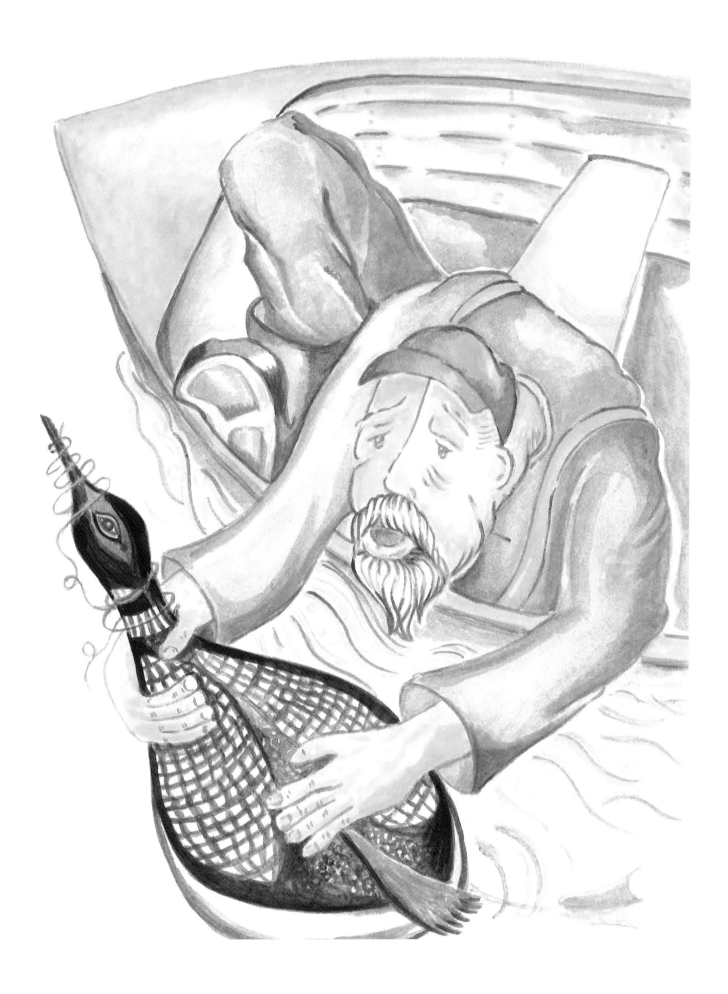

Relieved that Mr. Brown isn't choking the bird, Jason races up to his camp to retrieve some scissors. Mr. Brown rows the boat closer to shore with one hand while still holding onto the loon with the other. Those crimson colored eyes speak to him.

"I'm doing the best I can. Remember, I didn't ask to be your savior!" he mutters to the silent loon. When Jason returns to the shore, the young boy can't believe what he sees!

"Wow! This loon is gigantic!" exclaims Jason as he wades into the lake until he reaches the side of Mr. Brown's boat.

"And she's strong too. So stop jabbering and start snipping at this fishing line. I don't know how long she's gonna let me hold onto her."

Jason is worried. He's afraid he might cut the bird by accident, so he starts to talk. That's what he does when he's nervous. Hearing his own voice sort of calms him down. "Did you know that loons have four different calls, and each one means something different?" Jason asks while he carefully begins cutting the line away from the loon.

"No kidding? I just thought they squawked a lot to annoy me!" Otis replies with a wink. With Jason's help, Mr. Brown carefully unwinds the fishing line. Jason is amazed that all the while the loon is at ease in the old man's grasp.

Finally, the loon is free. The old man gently releases his steady grip on the bird and Jason watches her swim away effortlessly. Jason knows these birds are designed to swim. They are awkward fliers, and believe it or not, they are safest in the water. Still he has to ask, "Do you think she's okay?"

"Well, she's better off than she was, that's for sure," Mr. Brown grunts. "Probably starving, tangled up like that for who knows how long."

A few days later Jason notices the old man sitting on his dock with his feet dangling in the cool lake water. *It's a perfect day for fishing,* the young boy thinks. He runs down the hill, tackle box and pole in hand. He quietly sits down next to his neighbor, clumsily casts his line and waits in silence. Before too long Jason sees his bobber disappear underneath the water, then feels a tug on his pole.

"I got a bite, I got a bite!" he yells. Otis smiles.

"Set the hook, kid. Now reel her in nice and steady." Jason struggles with the pole. He has gotten his hook caught on something on the bottom of the lake: an old log, some rocks, or maybe some trash.

"Take it easy. Don't snap the line." Otis slowly eases himself into the lake and wades out to the end of the fishing line. He pulls and tugs, moves a few rocks out of the way. Eventually the hook is free. Jason reels the line in and sets the pole down on the dock.

Otis returns and sits next to his young neighbor. They sit together for a while in silence, just the way Mr. Brown likes it. A splash in the water catches their attention. Ten yards from the dock a loon slowly swims by.

"That's our loon," Jason says matter-of-factly. Then, Jason gets up, grabs his pole and heads up to his camp. His mom is calling him for dinner.

Otis watches him scramble up the hill. He turns back to face the lake and sees the loon raise herself up out of the water, flap her wings, and let out a beautiful call. It is the wail, the most frequently heard call of the loon, used when one loon is trying to locate another.

You may be right kid, Mr. Brown says to himself. *You just may be right.*

Thank you to my camp neighbor, Jim Langford. While he is not a 10 year old boy, Jim's assistance in freeing the loon allowed me to create another character in my story.

A special thanks to Jim's wife, Molly Aldrich, who captured the event on film.

A native of Bethesda, Maryland, Virginia Cassarino-Brown moved to Maine 28 years ago with her husband, Allan. They reside in Harpswell and have two grown children, Jason and Jordan. Virginia has written stories for the magazine, *Adventures for the Average Woman* and *Thin Threads: More Real Stories for Life Changing Moments. The Tangled Loon* is her first children's book. She is currently working on another.

Dawn Leeman Prindall has happily "doodled" throughout life working as an artist, a set-designer, a community liaison, an educator, a part-time waitress and more. Kids and community are incredibly important to Dawn and she is dedicated to both, volunteering for numerous groups. Whatever endeavor Dawn pursues, she is inspired by life on Orr's Island, Maine and by her vibrant friends and family. She is thrilled to be accompanied by her true love, Dave, and two very great (and nearly grown) sons, Sam and Tim. Dawn's motto: Make the world a little better, each and every day.

Maine Audubon works to conserve Maine's wildlife and wildlife habitat by engaging people of all ages in education, conservation and action. The Maine Loon Project was started by Maine Audubon in 1983 to monitor Maine's loon population over time, to deliver education and outreach programs to the public, and to advocate for healthy lakes and clean water in Maine's legislature. If you would like to learn more about loons and how to protect them, visit **http://www.maineaudubon.org/conserve/loon/index.shtml**

CPSIA information can be obtained
at www.ICGtesting.com
Printed in the USA
254256LV00003B

9781597131186